This book
belongs to:

Text written by Gill Davies/Illustrated by Tina Freeman
First published in Great Britain in 2001 by Brimax
an imprint of Octopus Publishing Group Ltd
2-4 Heron Quays, London, E14 4JP
© Octopus Publishing Group Ltd

Lucy Lamb

BRIMAX READ WITH ME

Lucy Lamb

It is Spring on Yellow Barn Farm.

"Moo!" says Mrs Cow. "I hear
that the bluebells in Ferny Wood
are wonderful this year."

"Baa!" says Lucy Lamb.
"I should like to hear them."

So Lucy trots along the lane until she comes to Ferny Wood.

Then Lucy stands. She looks around and listens.

Lucy can see lots of beautiful blue flowers swaying gently in the breeze.

But she cannot hear any bells!

Just then, Foxy Cub peeps through the trees.

"Where do the bluebells ring?" asks Lucy.

"I don't know," says Foxy, "but I should like to hear them."

So Lucy trots further into the wood and Foxy Cub scampers after her.

Just then, Squirrel peeps through the leaves.

"Do you know where the bluebells ring?" asks Lucy.

"No," says Squirrel, "but it would be fun to find out."

So Lucy trots further into the wood, and Foxy Cub and Squirrel scamper after.

Just then, Sukie Rabbit peeps through the bracken.

"Do the bluebells ring here?" asks Lucy.

"I have no idea," says Sukie, "but I should like to know."

So Lucy trots further into the wood, and Foxy, Squirrel and Sukie scamper after her.

Just then, Oliver Otter scrambles up the river bank. He wants to know what all the trotting and scampering is about!

"Can you tell us where the bluebells ring?" asks Lucy.

Oliver begins to smile. His smile gets wider and wider, and then he begins to laugh.

"Bluebells don't ring," laughs Oliver, rolling on the grass and holding his tummy.

"They are flowers. They are all around you. Look!"

The animals look at the bell shapes of the beautiful blue flowers.

Then they look back at Oliver rolling on the grass.

Very soon, Lucy, Foxy, Squirrel and Sukie are rolling on the grass and laughing, too!

When all the animals stop laughing, they all agree that Mrs Cow is right about the bluebells…

They are really wonderful this year!

Here are some words in the story. Can you read them?

farm	otter
wood	bluebells
lamb	Spring
trees	trots
squirrel	ring
fox	river
rabbit	cow

How much of the story can you remember?

Who tells Lucy Lamb that the bluebells in Ferny Wood are wonderful this year?

Lucy can't hear the bells in Ferny Wood, but what can she see lots of?

Which three animals help Lucy to find the bluebells?

What are their names?

Who tells Lucy and her friends that bluebells are flowers?

Can you spot five differences
in these pictures?

Notes for parents

The Yellow Barn Farm stories will help to expand your child's vocabulary and reading skills.

Key words are listed in each of the books and are repeated several times - point them out along with the corresponding illustrations as you read the story. The following ideas for discussion will expand on the things your child has read and learnt about on the farm, and will make the experience of reading more pleasurable.

• What kinds of animals live on Yellow Barn Farm? Ask your child to point to them in the illustrations.

• Make a "Moo!" sound and a "Baa!" sound. Ask your child to do the same!

• Talk about the different types of animals that Lucy meets in Ferny Wood.

• Are there any squirrels or rabbits that live near you?
Point them out to your child so they can bridge the gap between books and reality, which will help to make books all the more real.